W9-CAX-498

The WILD SWANS

by
Hans Christian Andersen

Illustrated by
Karen Milone

Troll Associates

Library of Congress Cataloging in Publication Data

Andersen, Hans Christian, 1805-1875.
   The wild swans.

   Translation of De vilde svaner.
   SUMMARY: Eleven brothers who have been turned into
swans by their evil stepmother are saved by their beau-
tiful sister.
   [1. Swans—Fiction. 2. Fairy tales] I. Milone,
Karen. II. Title.
PZ8.A542Wi 1981   [Fic]   80-27685
ISBN 0-89375-480-3
ISBN 0-89375-481-1 (pbk.)

The WILD SWANS

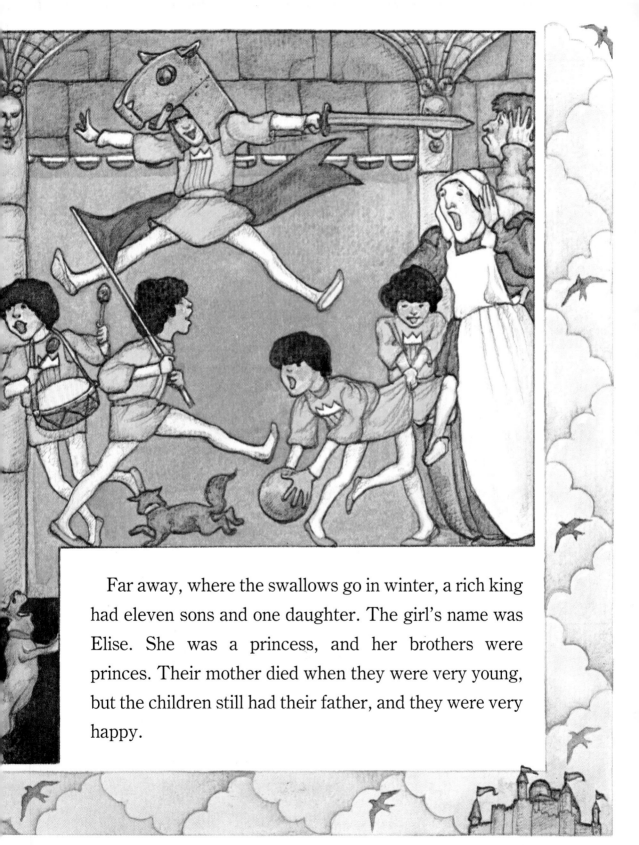

Far away, where the swallows go in winter, a rich king had eleven sons and one daughter. The girl's name was Elise. She was a princess, and her brothers were princes. Their mother died when they were very young, but the children still had their father, and they were very happy.

Then one day, the king married a wicked queen. She sent Elise to live with some peasants. Then she turned the boys into wild swans and sent them out into the world.

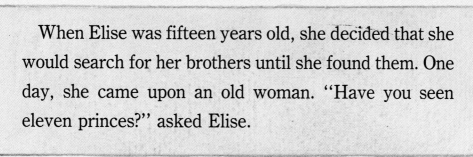

When Elise was fifteen years old, she decided that she would search for her brothers until she found them. One day, she came upon an old woman. "Have you seen eleven princes?" asked Elise.

"No," replied the woman. "But I did see eleven swans with golden crowns. They were swimming in that stream."

Elise followed the stream until it reached the ocean. Late that afternoon, she saw eleven swans with golden crowns. They flew toward shore and landed. Then, as the sun slipped below the horizon, the swans lost their feathers and turned into eleven handsome princes. They were Elise's brothers!

They told her that the wicked queen had cast a spell on them. Each day, when the sun came up, they became wild swans. And each night, when the sun set, they became princes again. They were only in this land for a visit. Soon, they would return to the cave where they lived—far across the sea. "Come with us!" they cried. "We will weave a net in which to carry you!" And Elise agreed.

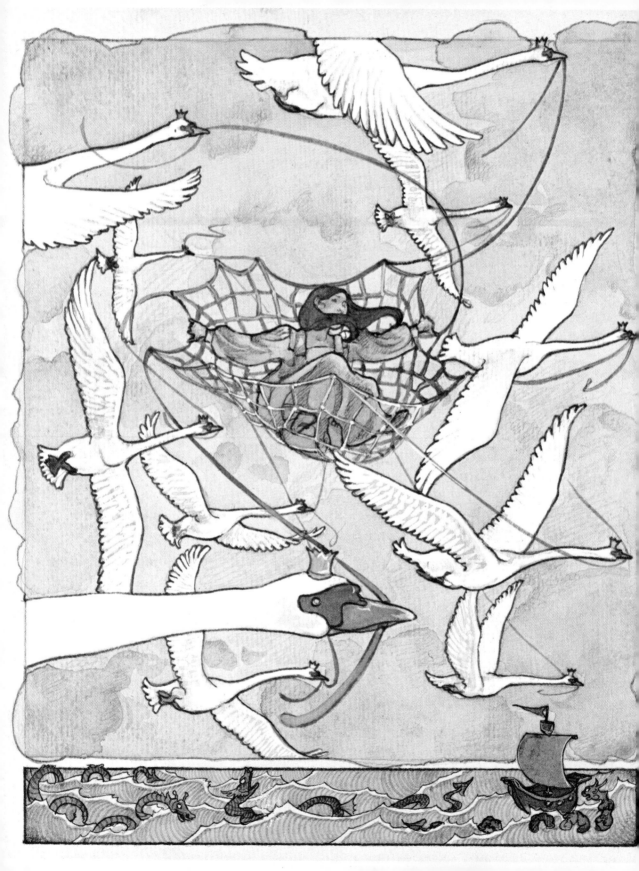

So they worked all night, and by morning, the net was finished. The wild swans lifted Elise into the air and flew out across the ocean. All day long, they flew high above the waves. The ocean was too wide to cross in one day, so they had to stop halfway across. They knew of a rock that stuck out of the middle of the sea. But they had to reach it before nightfall. For when the sun set, the swans would become princes again. If they were still in the sky, they would fall into the sea and drown.

As they flew, Elise could not see the rock. The sun dropped lower in the sky, and still there was no sign of the rock. A storm began to brew, and the waves seemed to reach up for them. The swans flew on and on. Suddenly, they dropped down and landed on the rock. The sun was just setting.

All night, the sister and her brothers clung to each other, as the storm raged around them. When the sun rose in the morning, the storm ended. The princes became swans again and continued their journey. Finally, they reached a distant shore. That night, as Elise slept in the cave that was her brothers' home, she had a strange dream.

In her dream, a fairy appeared, saying, "You can break the queen's spell and free your brothers. First, you must pick the stinging nettles that grow outside this cave. Only these nettles—or the ones found in churchyards—will do. You must stamp on them with your bare feet until they are like flax. Then you must make thread, and use it to weave eleven shirts. If you throw the shirts over the swans, the spell will be broken. But if you speak one word before all this is done, your brothers will die."

When Elise awoke, she saw the nettles outside the cave. Without a word, she set to work, though the nettles stung her hands and feet. That night, when her brothers returned, Elise refused to speak. She worked all night, and all the next day. By sunset, she had finished the first of the eleven shirts.

The following day, as she was weaving, some hunters happened to see her. The handsomest hunter was a king. He asked her many questions, but Elise would not speak. "This is no place for anyone so lovely," said the king, and he took her to his palace.

Elise was dressed in velvets and silks, but she was not happy. The king did everything he could to win her love. One day, he led her to a room that was made to look like the cave in which she had lived. In the room were the nettles she had picked, and the shirt she had already sewn. At once, a smile came to her lips.

Shortly after, the silent princess became the queen of the entire country. But every night, while the king slept, Elise went into the room that looked like the cave. There she continued to make the shirts that would set her brothers free.

Break the nettles. Comb the fibers. Spin the thread.

Weave the cloth. Cut the pattern. Sew the shirt.

Soon she had used the last of the nettles. At midnight, she sneaked outside and went to the churchyard. She passed the spirits that lived in the graveyard, and quickly, she picked more nettles. Then she returned to the palace.

No one saw her except a wicked counselor, who told the king that Elise was a witch. He said that she was using magic to cast a spell over the king and his country.

That night, the king pretended to go to sleep. He listened as Elise got out of bed and went into the room that looked like a cave. She stamped on the nettles, made the thread, and sat down to weave. Night after night, she returned to her weaving. And when all the shirts were finished except one, she again ran out of nettles.

At midnight, when Elise stole outside, the king and his counselor followed her to the churchyard. The king saw Elise enter the graveyard. He did not know she was only looking for more nettles. He thought she was visiting the spirits. "Let her be judged by the people," ordered the king.

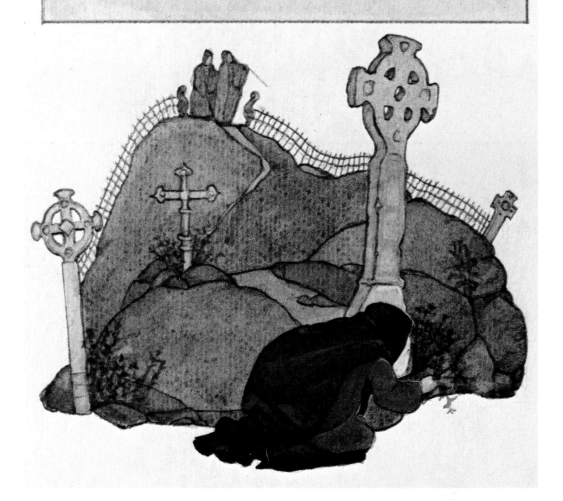

The people said that Elise was a witch and should be burned at the stake in the morning. Elise spent the night in a cold dungeon. Instead of smooth sheets for her bed, she was given the stinging nettles she had picked. Instead of soft blankets, she was given the ten shirts she had sewn.

And so, through the night, she was able to continue her work.

Morning came, and still she was sewing the last shirt. How her fingers flew! She had not yet finished it when they brought her to the village square, where she would be put to death. All the townspeople mocked her. They tried to take the shirts from her. But eleven white swans suddenly rushed down, beating their wings, and drove the people back.

As she was taken to the stake, Elise threw the shirts over the eleven swans. And in their places stood eleven princes. Elise had not finished the last of the shirts, so the youngest prince still had one swan's wing.

"Now I can speak!" cried Elise. "I am innocent!" And then she fainted.

The oldest brother told the king all that had taken place. As he spoke, red roses blossomed around Elise. There was also a single white rose, which the king picked. He held it out to Elise, and she immediately awakened.

Then bells began to ring, and birds flew through the skies. And peace and happiness spread throughout the land.